The grueling days and nights seemed to have no end. But finally, *Neptune's Car* rounded Cape Horn and sailed into the Pacific Ocean. The sails filled with wind and sped the ship northward.

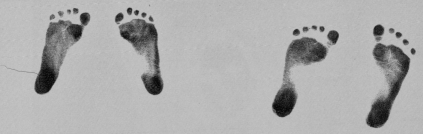

For Georgie and Benedict

First published 2000
This edition published 2002
By Egmont Books Limited
239 Kensington High Street, London W8 6SA
Text and illustrations copyright © Melanie Walsh 2000
Melanie Walsh has asserted her moral rights
A CIP catalogue record for this title is available from the British Library
ISBN 0 7497 4430 8
Printed in Hong Kong
1 3 5 7 9 10 8 6 4 2

Do Donkeys Dance?

Melanie Walsh

EGMONT

Do pigs buzz
around flowers?

No, bees buzz around flowers.

Can a turtle bounce ?

No, but Kangaroos
can, very high!

Can a cat hang
upside down
in a tree?

No, but bats can.

Do hippos hop?

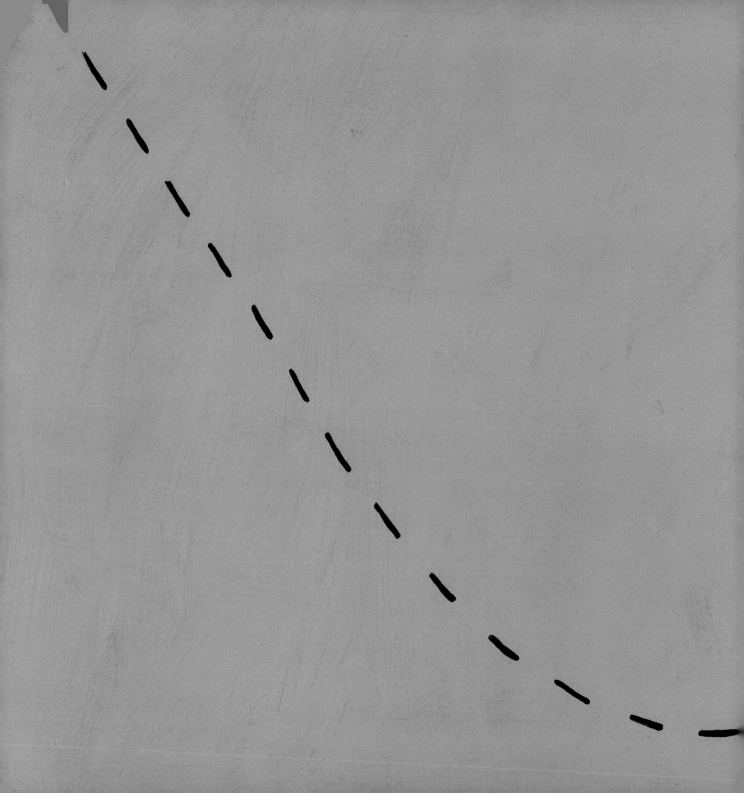

No, but fleas do.

Do chickens swim
under the sea?

No, fish do.

Can ladybirds stand
on one leg?

No, but flamingos can.

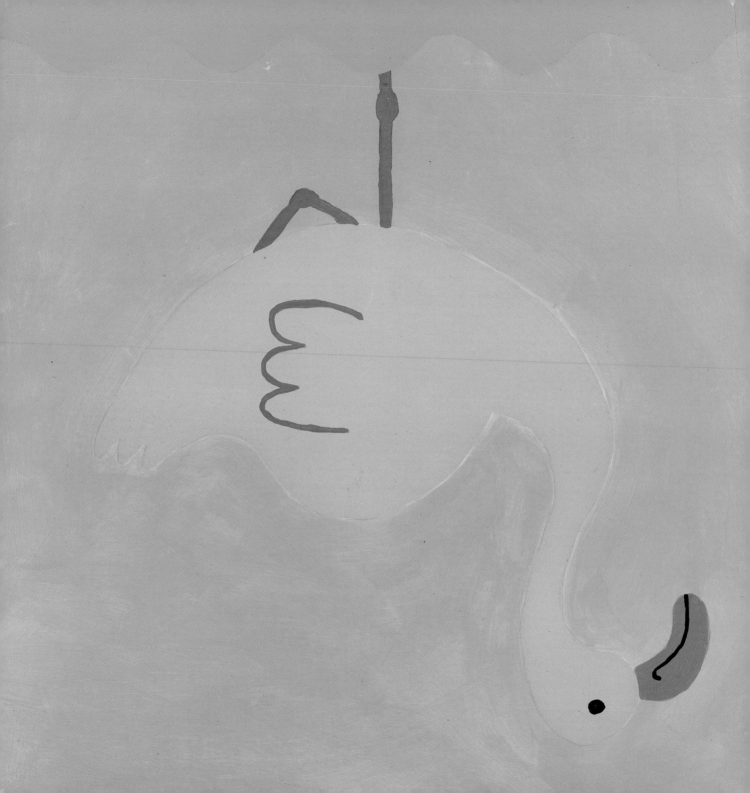

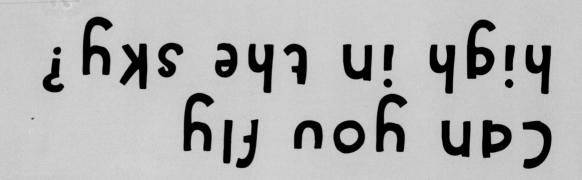

Can you fly
high in the sky?

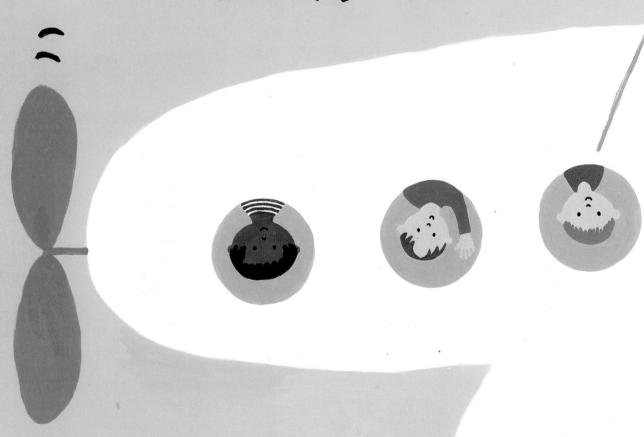

MADE BY **EGMONT**

HANDLED WITH CARE

Books are great! And these ones prove it.
goose **Wolf**

Koala and the Flower by Mary Murphy
0 7497 4407 3

I Don't Want to Sleep Alone
by Alison Ritchie and Cathy Gale
0 7497 4661 0

A Story for Hippo
by Simon Puttock and Alison Bartlett
0 7497 4022 1

Mr Wolf's Pancakes by Jan Fearnley
0 7497 3559 7

Cat's Colours by Jane Cabrera
0 7497 3120 6

Dog's Day by Jane Cabrera
0 7497 4392 1

I wish I were a dog by Lydia Monks
0 7497 3803 0

The Three Little Wolves and the Big Bad Pig
by Eugene Trivizas and Helen Oxenbury
0 7497 2505 2

And they're all only £4.99